THE MAN OF STEEL

THE POISONED PLANET

WRITTEN BY
MATTHEW K. MANNING

ILLUSTRATED BY
LUCIANO VECCHIO

SUPERMAN CREATED BY
JERRY SIEGEL AND
JOE SHUSTER
BY SPECIAL ARRANGEMENT WITH
THE JERRY SIEGEL FAMILY

RAINTREE IS AN IMPRINT OF CAPSTONE GLOBAL LIBRARY
LIMITED, A COMPANY INCORPORATED IN ENGLAND AND
WALES HAVING ITS REGISTERED OFFICE AT 264 BANBURY
ROAD, OXFORD, OX2 7DY -REGISTERED COMPANY NUMBER:
6695582

WWW.RAINTREE.CO.UK
MYORDERS@RAINTREE.CO.UK

APPLICATIONS FOR THE COPYRIGHT OWNER'S WRITTEN
PERMISSION SHOULD BE ADDRESSED TO THE PUBLISHER.

ART DIRECTOR: BOB LENTZ AND BRANN GARVEY
DESIGNER: HILARY WACHOLZ

ISBN 978 1 4747 3284 0
20 19 18 17 16
10 9 8 7 6 5 4 3 2 1

BRITISH LIBRARY CATALOGUING IN PUBLICATION DATA
A FULL CATALOGUE RECORD FOR THIS BOOK IS AVAILABLE
FROM THE BRITISH LIBRARY.

PRINTED AND BOUND IN CHINA

CONTENTS

Years ago, in a distant galaxy, the planet Krypton exploded. Its only survivor was a baby called Kal-El who escaped in a rocket ship. After landing on Earth, he was adopted by the Kents, a kind couple who named him Clark. The boy soon discovered he had extraordinary abilities fuelled by the yellow sun of Earth. He chose to use these powers to help others, and so he became Superman - the guardian of his new home.

He is...

CHAPTER 1

GOING GREEN WITH IVY

Danny was tired of walking. He'd been lugging his heavy backpack for nearly four hours now. The air was so humid in the jungle that he had started sweating the moment he left his cabin. He'd been sweating ever since.

Another thick entanglement of vines blocked his path. Danny paused for a moment and took a deep, heavy breath.

"Keep moving up there," came his boss' voice from behind him.

Danny sighed and wondered why his boss didn't ever seem to need a rest. It was like she thrived out here in the wild.

"Let's go, kid," said the man standing directly behind Danny. Ron nudged Danny forward with his elbow as if to make his point. "You heard the lady."

Danny weakly reached into his backpack. He felt around for a moment or two. Then he slid a long machete out of its outer pocket. He raised the long knife in his hands and focused on the vines.

"No!" screamed his boss. Danny turned around as his boss pushed her way past the other men to the front of the line. "How many times do I have to tell you?" she said. "You will not harm any plants!"

The woman slid past Danny. He glanced over at Ron, who was smiling. He seemed to be enjoying himself a little too much. Danny turned back to face their boss. Surprisingly, she had somehow parted the tangled vines. In fact, she was already a long way ahead of him.

Danny slid his machete back into his backpack.

"Move it," said Ron from behind him.

"Okay, okay," Danny said. He looked back at his older partner. He had worked with Ron for years now, and every time it was the same. Ron was always grumpy and rude. After all the jobs they'd done together, Danny assumed they would be friends by now. But if Ron even had any friends, Danny was certainly not one of them.

When Danny turned back around, his boss was nowhere to be seen. It was as if she'd just disappeared into the thick brush of the jungle.

"Where did she –?" Danny started to say under his breath. Then he thought better of it. He decided his time would be better spent trying to catch up to his employer. So Danny started to jog.

The path was just too overgrown with weeds and ferns for him to move very quickly. Nevertheless, he did his best. The last thing he wanted to do now was get his boss even more annoyed with him. This was the first job he had had in months, and he didn't know when another would come along.

Danny pushed past a particularly sharp, thorny tree of some kind. Then he stopped.

t of Danny was a clearing. The rays hit his face and neck. He squinted in the bright light. There, a couple of metres ahead of him, was a trench several metres below ground level.

Danny walked over and peered down into the hole. His boss had already beaten him there. She was down in the crater, kneeling in front of a strange glowing rock. She had taken off her hat. Danny noticed her long and flowing red hair. It looked out of place there, surrounded by all the green vegetation and the green stone in front of her. Even her skin seemed to have a greenish tint to it. Danny had never noticed that before.

"Is everything okay?" he asked.

His boss laughed.

But it didn't sound like something was funny. It was a dark little chuckle. Then she said, "Everything is perfect."

It was hard to see in the bright sunlight, but Danny could make out something in his boss' hands. She was holding the end of a long vine. The vine was growing right out of the earth under the glowing rock in the crater. Just like the strange stone, the plant was glowing bright green.

"I think we found what we were looking for," said Danny's boss. She stood up and faced him. Danny could hear the rest of the men spreading out behind him in the clearing. It was time to get to work. And even in the heat and humidity, no one was about to protest.

Danny had kept his complaints to himself for the last few hours. He'd rather be miserable than make his boss angry.

One thing he had learned over the past few days – he did not want to get on Poison Ivy's bad side.

*   *   *

KAPOWWWWWWWWWWWW!

Superman smacked Parasite with a giant telephone pole. The villain was sent crashing into a concrete wall with a **THUDDDD!** He was unconscious.

Finally, Superman thought. *Fighting a villain you can't touch is tiring.*

Superman had been forced to take a rather long lunch break to hunt down Parasite, a power-sucking super-villain.

Cautiously, Superman picked up the unconscious Parasite by his collar and soared into the air.

FWOOOOOOOOOOOOOSH!

Just another day as the Man of Steel, Superman thought.

Moments later, he was dropping off the unconscious super-villain at Slab Maximum Penitentiary. After talking with the guards and explaining the situation, he leaped into the air and soared towards his day job at the *Daily Planet* newspaper.

As he touched down on the rooftop of the Daily Planet Building, the hero just hoped no one would notice. It wasn't exactly Superman who would get into trouble. It was his alter ego, reporter Clark Kent, who would have to face an angry boss if he was discovered.

Perry White was a fair boss, but he was pretty strict about punctuality. And Clark Kent couldn't explain that Superman had been forced to fight the Parasite on the outskirts of the city, then fly to the Slab Maximum Penitentiary to ensure that the super-villain wouldn't escape again.

If Superman told anyone why he was late, then that would mean everyone would know he was Clark Kent. If the world found out that Clark and Superman were the same person, everyone he had ever met would become targets of Superman's countless enemies. And Superman refused to put other people at risk.

So, Superman changed into Clark Kent's work clothes in the shadow of the revolving globe on the rooftop of the Daily Planet.

Clark Kent would get a stern lecture from his boss, but there was nothing even the Man of Steel could do about it.

Clark opened the rooftop door. He walked down the two flights of stairs to the Daily Planet Building's newsroom floor. He walked past the main elevators and began to head down the corridor towards the newsroom and his desk. But as he approached the end of the corridor and the glass double doors that led to the newsroom, he noticed an odd smell with his enhanced senses: the scent of lilacs.

At first Clark assumed he had forgotten someone's birthday. One of his co-workers must have received a bouquet for the special occasion. As Clark reached the doors, he quickly moved out of view of anyone in the main newsroom.

Clark looked at the wall in front of him and used his X-ray vision. Inside, he could see four men holding cattle prods.

That's not good, Clark thought.

He scanned the rest of the room. No one was hurt. But even so, everyone looked terrified. He could see his friend Jimmy Olsen, his boss Perry White and even Lois Lane. Clark exhaled a sigh of relief that Lois was safe. Now it was time to get to work.

Clark concentrated and used his super-hearing. He could hear a woman's voice. It sounded familiar to him. He knew the person talking, but he couldn't quite place the voice.

". . . has gone on long enough," said the woman.

Clark searched the room and zeroed in on the speaker. She was a red-headed woman wearing a green, leafy uniform. He recognized her instantly as Batman's old enemy, Poison Ivy.

"I don't know what you're talking about," said Perry White. He was facing Ivy. He looked scared and frustrated.

"Do you have any idea what kind of impact you're having on the world?" asked Poison Ivy.

Clark noticed that she looked even angrier than usual. Whenever they had met, she was always plotting some deadly campaign to save Mother Nature. She saw herself as the spokesperson for all plant life. She viewed humans as her enemies, and hated them for slowly killing the planet with their pollution and waste.

Poison Ivy was constantly using her plant-controlling abilities to try and destroy all human life on Earth. Needless to say, considering her beliefs and the state of the world today, the villain had very little to smile about.

"Ninety-five million trees are murdered by the newspaper industry every year," Poison Ivy was saying in the other room. "Your business creates millions of tonnes of greenhouse gases and wastewater."

Perry White didn't respond. He seemed genuinely surprised by what Ivy was saying.

"Considering that, I think it's safe to say that newspapers are an enemy of nature," said Poison Ivy. "So you've made an enemy of me."

Perry White put his hands up in front of him. "Let's talk about this," he said. "No one needs to get hurt here."

"It's a little too late for that," said Ivy.

Clark had heard enough. He didn't want to waste time by heading back to the roof to change. So he quickly jogged to the opposite end of the corridor. He threw open the door to the supply room.

The small cupboard-like room was filled with items such as paperclips and reams of paper. Due to its convenient location, and the fact that it had a lock on the inside of its door, the room was the perfect place for Clark to change into Superman's uniform. Even better, it also had a small window on its far wall, making Superman's quick exits even quicker.

As Clark unbuttoned his shirt to reveal the famous S-shield underneath, he felt the start of a headache coming on. To most people, the mild pain would be nothing new. But not to Superman. Unlike most people, Superman didn't get headaches.

The Man of Steel decided to ignore the pain for now. Instead, the hero once again used his super-hearing. He concentrated and homed in on Poison Ivy's voice.

". . . fifteen minutes to make the arrangements," Poison Ivy was saying. "By the end of that time, the *Daily Planet* had better have made the switch to 100% recycled paper."

"I understand what you're saying," came a voice from across the newsroom. Superman knew that voice all too well. It was Lois's. "And I agree with you."

Superman looked towards the newsroom using his X-ray vision again. Lois was walking over to Poison Ivy. He was ready to move now, but he thought better of it. Lois was right next to Ivy. He didn't want to put her in harm's way.

"But it's not quite that simple," said Lois. "These things take time. And this certainly isn't the way to go about it."

"I don't remember asking for your opinion," said Poison Ivy.

"I'm just saying that there's a right way to do things and a wrong way," said Lois. "And taking hostages in Metropolis? In the Daily Planet Building of all places? That's just the wrong way."

"And why would that be?" asked Poison Ivy, annoyed.

Superman felt a sudden surge in the pain in his head again, then a weakness in his legs. He pushed it away and kept listening.

"This is Superman's city," said Lois. "*The* Superman. Maybe you've heard of him? Really strong guy? Leaps buildings in a single bound? Can knock out a crazy eco-terrorist without even breaking a sweat? Ring any bells?"

Poison Ivy grinned. "Why don't you look out the window?" she said. Lois narrowed her eyes at her. Then she turned to the row of windows lining the far wall. In all the excitement, she hadn't noticed what was growing on the outside of the building.

Superman looked over to the window of the supply room.

It was covered in strange glowing vines. They seemed to have sprouted up out of nowhere.

Superman walked over to the vines and opened the window. Immediately, he fell to his knees.

The green glow coming from the plants pulsed in the sunlight. It seemed to be sending shock waves of pain and weakness through Superman's entire body. It was all he could do to gather the strength to slam the window shut again.

It took all his focus to turn his super-hearing back to the newsroom. He could barely hear Ivy speaking.

"The vine itself isn't rare," Ivy said. "But the material I found it growing out of certainly is."

"Kryptonite," Lois said under her breath.

"Exactly," said Poison Ivy with a grin. "The vines feed on it. And as a result, this building is now overgrown with Kryptonite-laced vegetation."

ZIRRRRRRRRRRRRRT!

Superman used his X-ray vision to scan the exterior of the building. Poison Ivy wasn't exaggerating. The entire Daily Planet Building was now covered in a tangled mess of Kryptonite-infused vines.

"So Superman isn't much of an issue in this case," Poison Ivy said proudly. "He wouldn't be able to get past my vines even if his life depended on it."

Poison Ivy walked towards Lois and looked her straight in the eyes.

"But it's not his life I'd be worried about, if I were you," Poison Ivy warned. "Because if the *Daily Planet* newspaper doesn't meet my demands in the next fifteen minutes, everyone in this room is going to know the meaning of the words, 'print is dead'."

CHAPTER 2

ENERGY CONSERVATION

When Superman stumbled out of the supply room, he could barely keep his balance. It wasn't the most impressive entrance Superman had ever made in his career, but the Kryptonite surrounding the building had already weakened him. In a few more minutes, he wondered if he would even be able to stand up. Luckily, the Kryptonite wasn't in its purest form. Otherwise, Superman would probably be unconscious by now. Or worse.

Either way, Superman didn't expect an audience when he slammed the supply room door open. But that's exactly what he discovered. It seemed that two of Poison Ivy's men had left the main newsroom to patrol the building's corridors.

Superman tried to hide his nervousness. In his weakened state, he wasn't sure if he could handle the two thugs. He needed to conserve his strength the best he could, but he had no choice. He couldn't let these two report back to their boss. His only remaining advantage was the element of surprise.

Superman sprinted towards the closer of the two men. Amazingly, his super-speed was still working.

KAPOW!

It only took one punch to knock the first man to the floor.

Superman looked down at him. He was out cold. It seemed the Man of Steel still had a little fight left in him after all.

The other thug took one look at his fallen friend, then he ran towards the stairwell. Superman began to chase after him, but lost his balance.

THUMPPPPPPPP!

The hero fell to his knees. He tried to stand, but his legs felt like rubber bands. And he was far too weak to use his super-speed again.

Luckily, he had plenty of other powers to choose from. Superman focused his eyes on the door to the stairwell.

ZIRRRRRRRRRRRRRRRT!

The Man of Steel sent a burst of concentrated heat vision across the room.

SIZZZZZZZZZZZZZZZLE! The door's handle began to heat up. Then it slowly fused to the metal latch. When the henchman finally reached the door, not only was it too hot to touch, but it was welded completely shut.

CLANK! CLANK! CLANK! The man failed to pry open the door. Realizing he had nowhere else to go, he turned around to face his enemy.

Superman took one look at the thug, then simply said, "Don't move."

"Wha-what?" said the henchman.

"Stay right there," Superman said. Then he added, "Or else."

Superman calmly turned around and headed back to the supply room.

A short while later, he returned to the corridor. The criminal he'd left behind hadn't moved a muscle. He had seen what Superman could do. It was obvious that the crook was terrified.

Superman walked towards him. It was more of an effort than he let on. Every step filled him with pain. But Superman wasn't about to let his opponent know that.

The crook noticed that Superman was carrying a duffel bag over his shoulder with the *Daily Planet*'s logo on it. The bag looked full, but the criminal had no idea what was in it. But that only made his fear of the bag's contents that much greater.

When he was a metre away from the criminal, Superman reached inside the bag. "Here," he said calmly. He removed a long plastic zip tie he'd found in the supply room. "Put your hands behind your back right now."

The criminal did exactly what he was told as fast as he could. *ZIPPPPPPPP!* Superman wrapped the man's wrists with the plastic tie. Then he ran it through the door's handle. *ZIPPPPPPPP!* He fastened the tie and pulled it snugly. There was no way he could escape.

Superman frowned at the now incapacitated criminal. "How many of you are there?" he asked.

"Of us?" said the criminal. He didn't even try to withhold the information. This was Superman he was talking to.

"There're five of us on this floor," the criminal admitted. "I mean, if you count Ivy, that is. And she's got two guards on the front door downstairs. But that's everyone."

"You're not lying to me, are you?" asked Superman. He stared at the man, locking the criminal's eyes with his own.

"N-no," said the trembling thug. "I swear!"

Superman glared at the criminal. He realized the whole time he was tying the crook's hands, he was breathing heavily. Even this conversation was taking a lot out of him.

Superman put his bag down on the ground and knelt by it. He tried to keep his breathing under control as he moved.

When Superman stood back up, he was holding a white tablecloth in his hands. Superman strained with nearly all his strength as he ripped a narrow strip of the cloth. **RRRRRRRRRIP!** His arms were shaking by the time he'd finished tearing the sheet to shreds.

"Hey, man," said the henchman. "What's wrong with you?"

Superman tied the cloth around the man's mouth, making sure it was tight. He didn't want either of these men letting Poison Ivy know he was there.

Even more importantly, he didn't want Poison Ivy to know how weak he was.

Superman picked his bag up. He grunted as he headed towards the other, unconscious, thug.

Superman used another zip tie to fasten the man to the radiator. Then he tied a gag around that man's mouth as well.

He walked slowly over to the elevator and pushed the DOWN button. **CLICK!**

Superman leaned against the wall as he waited for the elevator. He knew the criminal down the corridor was watching him, but it didn't matter now. The Man of Steel needed to conserve all the strength he could.

DING!

The elevator doors opened on the first floor lobby of the Daily Planet Building. The Man of Steel stood up straight. The super hero stepped out of the elevator and into the lobby.

The two security guards at the opposite side of the room looked amazed. Although he'd been in Metropolis for years, Superman still wasn't a common sight.

The two men stayed where they were behind the desk as he walked slowly across the floor. They kept their wide eyes on Superman the whole time, unable to look away.

"Excuse me, gentlemen," said Superman. "Is everything okay down here?"

"Um . . . uh, yes!" said the first guard. And then added, "Sir."

Superman looked over at the double doors. The glowing vines were all that could be seen through their windows.

Looks like I can't get in through here, either, Superman thought. The second guard noticed what Superman was looking at.

"Well, except for the vines," he said. "They're so thick, no one can get in or out. They just started growing out of nowhere."

"You haven't seen any suspicious people?" asked Superman. "No one's come down here lately?"

"No, sir," said the second guard.

Superman looked over at the first guard again. He seemed to be rather nervous. The guard dabbed his sleeve on his forehead.

Superman looked down at the desk in front of him.

Underneath, there was an overturned coffee cup resting against the desk's inside wall. Superman watched a drop of coffee fall to the floor. **DRIP! DRIP! DRIP!**

Then Superman looked lower to the ground. He used his X-ray vision to see directly through the desk.

There, hidden from view, were two men. Each had been stripped of his guard's jacket and hat. Superman watched as another drop of coffee fell on one of the guard's shoes.

DRIP! DRIP! The sound was as loud as thunder to someone with super-hearing like Superman.

Superman looked back up at the first guard. "You spilled your coffee," Superman said slowly.

The crook pretending to be a guard swallowed hard. He made a loud gulping sound. And then suddenly, he pulled a taser gun out of his jacket and pointed it at Superman's chest. So did his partner in crime.

"D-don't move," the other man stuttered, aiming the taser at Superman's chest.

Superman looked over to the first guard. He had his taser aimed at him, as well – pointed at Superman's famous S-shield.

Superman did his best to control his emotions. He was having a hard enough time standing up straight, so disarming these men was completely out of the question. He was too weak for a fight, and too slow to stop them.

Even worse, in Superman's current state, these tasers could quite possibly kill him if they both struck him at once.

If Superman was going to survive, he needed to think fast. "Really?" he said. "You're going to shoot me? The Man of Steel? With a taser?"

Neither crook said anything. The first crook looked uncertainly at his partner.

"You do know that even bullets bounce right off me, right?" asked Superman.

The crooks remained silent. "If you fire those guns," Superman said, "you won't hurt me. You'll just make me angry."

The first crook's hand started to shake.

Superman reached into the *Daily Planet* duffle bag over his shoulder and pulled out two zip ties.

Then he placed the zip ties on the desk. "Now, if you don't want to make me angry," he said in a grim voice, "take these zip ties and cuff yourselves to the front door."

The two crooks looked at each other for a moment. And then they looked at the tasers in their hands. They dropped their weapons down on the desk and quickly picked up the zip ties. Then they walked over to the double doors and hastily cuffed each other to their handles.

"You made the right choice," said Superman. Then he collapsed to the floor.

At least three minutes passed before Superman woke up. The Kryptonite was too much for him. He had never felt this weak in his life.

Superman slowly picked himself up off the floor. He grabbed his bag, headed over to the elevator, and pushed the UP button.

CLICK!

Once inside the elevator, he caught a glimpse of the two fake guards before the doors closed. They were still safely cuffed. They looked even more surprised now than when they had first seen him.

Superman wiped the perspiration from his brow. *Can't blame them for being surprised,* he thought. *Not many people get to see Superman sweat.*

CHAPTER 3

ENERGY CRISIS

Danny was bored. He thought for certain that this part of the job would be fun and exciting. But so far, he'd spent this whole trip to the Daily Planet Building just waiting for something to happen.

Danny thought that was probably a good thing. Poison Ivy had planned this mission perfectly. If she hadn't, it would be more exciting. But that's because they would have to face Superman. And that's something no criminal ever wanted to do.

"Your time is up, Mr White," said Poison Ivy from across the room.

Danny looked over at his boss. Then he looked over at his partner, Ron. Both of them were smiling. It looked like Danny's boredom was about to end.

"Please," said Perry White. He was standing by a desk and holding a telephone up to his ear. "I'm still on hold with the printer. This kind of thing doesn't just happen right away."

Poison Ivy chuckled. "That's why I gave you fifteen minutes," she said. "Let's show Mr White how serious we are, okay, boys?" Poison Ivy looked over at Jimmy Olsen. "That one. Superman's pal. Let's see how well he flies without his best friend around."

Danny knew a command when he
heard one. This wasn't the type of thing he
liked to do, but he needed the money. He
walked over to Olsen. Ron followed him.
They both grabbed the young photographer
and dragged him over to a nearby open
window.

Poison Ivy stared at the window and
raised her eyebrows just slightly. The
vines outside parted. Danny started to
lift Jimmy into the air. And then he felt a
hand tap lightly on his shoulder. Danny
looked behind him just in time to see a fist
smashing into his face.

POW!

Danny fell against the wall. He looked
up at the man in the red cape standing
over him.

It was Superman! Superman had punched him! Danny couldn't believe it. *How am I still awake?* he thought.

Suddenly, Superman slumped over. Danny watched as the Man of Steel leaned on a desk to keep himself from falling. He looked pale and he was sweating. This wasn't the Superman Danny had read about in the papers.

"That was just adorable," said Poison Ivy. She walked over to Superman. He straightened himself up and looked at her. He could barely stay standing.

KA·POWWWWW!

Poison Ivy punched Superman right in the stomach. The super hero doubled over and then fell to the ground. He looked like he was in terrible pain.

Poison Ivy smirked. "I've always wanted to do that," she said.

Danny couldn't believe it. No mere human could hurt Superman!

"Forget the original plan, boys," said Poison Ivy. "Let's make these people believe even the Man of Steel can break."

Danny stood back up and walked over to Superman. With Ron's help, they hoisted Superman up on their shoulders. They walked him over to the window. Superman was so weak, he could barely move. His head drooped from one side to the other.

Danny and Ron pushed Superman onto the window's ledge. Danny was excited. This was going to make his career. He'd never have trouble finding work again.

He would be the guy that destroyed Superman!

Ron grinned. He counted out loud. "One, two . . ."

"Three!" Danny said. Together, the two crooks pushed Superman out of the window.

The air rushing against his face brought Superman back to his senses. The Kryptonite had put him in a daze, but that didn't matter now. If he didn't act quickly, he'd be nothing more than a red and blue stain on the pavement.

Superman reached out his hands. He felt his fingertips brush against the Kryptonite vines as he fell. It stung with each touch, but that wasn't important. He had to save Lois and the others. He had to save them, no matter what the cost.

Superman reached out with his hand and snagged a piece of the vine. He tightened his grip as best he could. Miraculously, he held on. His body swung against the side of the building.

THUMP!

He hit the outside wall of the Daily Planet. The impact was enough to knock the wind out of the hero. But Superman held on despite his hand burning from the glowing Kryptonite plant.

He reached up with his other hand and grabbed another strand of the vine. His arms shook with pain, but below he could see a window. As luck would have it, there were only one or two vines sprawled across its surface. It wasn't covered as heavily as the rest of the building. His grip was growing weaker by the second.

The intense pain shot up his arms to his chest as Superman kicked back against the building with all his strength. His body swung forwards again. And then he let go.

CRASH!

His body shot forwards and shattered the glass window. He fell into the room and landed on an empty desk with a *THUMP!* He slid off the desk and fell to the floor.

Superman's hands stung. His arms burned. He looked around at the deserted office. He wasn't sure what floor he was on, but at least he was alive.

Superman felt like he was going to be sick. His eyelids were heavy. He had never been so tired before.

He wondered if he could rest for a few moments before heading back upstairs to the newsroom.

He closed his eyes, and then he thought about Lois. He thought about Perry and Jimmy, and all his other co-workers.

Superman struggled back to his feet. It would have been easy to give in to sleep. But that wasn't the way Superman did things.

One of Ivy's thugs walked into the room. When he saw the struggling Superman leaning on a desk, he smiled wickedly. "I thought I heard something down here," he said. The crook raised his fists in front of him and cracked his knuckles. *POP! POP! POP!*

"I can't wait to tell all my friends that I beat up the Man of Steel!" the crook exclaimed.

Superman gathered every bit of strength he had left. He raised his fists in front of his face and gritted his teeth. "Let's see what you've got, tough guy," he said.

The criminal quickly circled to Superman's side. He dropped his shoulder and threw a hard right hook.

WOOOOOSH! Superman ducked just in time. The crook's punch sailed over his head.

Superman threw a quick kick to the crook's leg to knock the man off balance.

THUMP! The man landed hard on his side.

The crook immediately scrambled back to his feet. He looked quite surprised, but his fists remained clenched.

"You know," Superman said, trying hard to hide his growing weariness, "I've been fighting super-villains for years. Even without my superpowers, I've forgotten more about fighting than you'll ever know."

The thug's eyes went wide. He lowered his fists for a moment. That was the opening Superman needed.

WHAMMMM!

Superman's straight right punch connected with the man's exposed chin. It wasn't strong enough to seriously hurt the criminal, but it was enough to knock him to the ground with a *THUD!*

Struggling for breath, Superman jumped on the grounded crook and used his weight to hold him down. Then he reached towards a phone that had fallen off the desk and grabbed its cord.

Slowly, carefully, Superman bound the man's wrists and feet together.

"Sit tight," Superman said in a hoarse voice. Slowly, bracing himself against the wall, he made his way down the corridor towards the staircase.

CHAPTER 4
AIR POLLUTION

Even without his super-hearing, Superman could hear her voice echo down the hall.

"I've been nice about this, I really have," Poison Ivy said. As Superman limped closer to the newsroom, she continued her rant. "Can everyone see this? I want you to take a good look at this pouch in my hand."

The Man of Steel neared the glass doors to the newsroom.

Superman looked back over his shoulder at the two men he'd subdued earlier. Both were asleep.

Superman envied them for a moment. His body was telling him to do the exact same thing. Instead, he looked back towards the newsroom. Through the doors, he could see Poison Ivy standing next to Perry White. Perry looked terrified. And so did Lois.

"This pouch contains an airborne poison," he heard Poison Ivy say. "It's a little something I cooked up during one of my travels. If I empty this pouch into the air, you'll all fall asleep – and never wake up."

"We're trying to cooperate!" Lois said. "We're doing the best we can."

"The printer doesn't have the type of paper you asked for right now," Perry added. "Please, we just need a little more time –"

"I tried to play nice," said Poison Ivy. "But now it's too late. It's time to end this silly little newspaper."

"So that's the answer," Superman said as he pushed open the doors to the newsroom. He was talking more softly than usual. Even his voice was failing. He limped forwards, trying his best not to fall down. "Just kill everyone? That's your answer to the problem, Ivy?"

"I gave them a choice," said Poison Ivy. She was smiling at Superman, knowing full well that he was no longer a threat to her. She didn't even seem to care that he was still alive.

"Why are you doing this?" Superman asked. He stopped to lean on a desk and accidentally knocked a lamp off the edge. It hit the ground with a **CRUNCH!**

The noise startled Superman. After a moment, he forced himself to stand. "Who made you queen of the plant world?" he asked.

"I simply speak for those who cannot speak for themselves," said Ivy.

"Oh?" said Superman. "Have you even bothered to ask them what they think about all this?"

Poison Ivy laughed, and looked around the room. "Them?" she scoffed. "Why would I ask them? The *Daily Planet*'s employees are the biggest part of the problem!"

"I meant the newspapers themselves," said Superman, pointing at a stack of morning editions. "You can communicate with plant life, right? Well, at one time weren't those papers trees?"

Poison Ivy looked at Superman.

The Man of Steel slumped back over the desk. She almost felt sorry for the hero – almost. He just didn't know when to give up.

"You want me to talk to the newspapers?" Poison Ivy repeated. She took a step forward.

"Unless, like all bad rulers, you think you're above communicating with your own subjects," said Superman.

Poison Ivy's smile disappeared.

Poison Ivy didn't like being mocked. And that's exactly what Superman seemed to be doing to her. "I'm not their ruler," she said through gritted teeth. "I take care of them, and they take care of me."

Ivy was getting angry. Lois Lane shifted uncomfortably on her feet.

Poison Ivy's two henchmen stood in front of Lois, on the other side of a large desk. They both had their eyes on Superman, grinning at the struggling hero. They were so proud to be part of the crew that would finally bring down the Man of Steel.

Lois looked over to Jimmy Olsen. He returned her glance. Lois looked at the phone in front of him, and then at the lamp in front of her. Jimmy swallowed nervously, but nodded.

"Fine," Poison Ivy said. She walked over to a stack of papers by Perry White's office. "We'll see exactly what my kind thinks of the way yours treated them." She placed her hand on the stack of newspapers.

Poison Ivy stared off into space, concentrating very hard. Suddenly, her eyes rolled back in her head. "AHHHHH!!" she screamed.

"The pain!" Poison Ivy cried. "They've been through so much pain! So much suffering! It hurts!"

"Now!" Lois yelled. Jimmy picked up the heavy phone on the desk and Lois grabbed the lamp.

WHAM!

SMASH!

Jimmy hit the older thug in the head with the phone. At the exact same time, Lois smashed Danny with the lamp. The two henchmen collapsed to the floor, unconscious.

Lois looked over at Poison Ivy, ready to swing her weapon again. However, Ivy was on the ground now, lying motionless, with her eyes wide open. Poison Ivy seemed to be in some sort of trance.

She kept uttering, "No, no, no," over and over again.

It was as if Ivy was seeing something so terrible that she couldn't handle it. Whatever Ivy had felt when she reached out to listen to the newspapers, it had been far too much for her human mind to handle.

Lois looked over to the windows. The vines that had been blocking them were slowly receding.

Without Poison Ivy's influence, the vines were wilting and slowly dying.

Bit by bit, sunlight began to creep back into the room. And then, the vines withered completely.

CRUNCH!

Finally, they fell away from the building.

Lois let out a sigh of relief. It seemed that the worst of it was over now.

But then Lois looked over at Superman. He was no longer standing. He wasn't even slumped over the desk. In fact, just like Poison Ivy and her men, Superman was on the floor.

But his eyes weren't open, and he wasn't moving.

Even worse, the Man of Steel didn't seem to be breathing.

CHAPTER 5

CLIMATE CHANGE

Lois ran to the fallen super hero's side. She felt for his pulse, but couldn't tell for sure if his heart was still beating. "Superman, wake up!" she cried. "Why won't you wake up?"

Jimmy stood over Lois, uncertain what to do. Then he saw the withered vines hanging from the window sill.

Maybe there's still some Kryptonite in them! he thought.

Jimmy ran over to the window and began pulling on the vines. In a matter of seconds, the vines crumbled beneath his fingers. **CRUNCH! CRUNCH! CRUNCH!**

The vines fell away from the building, disintegrating before Jimmy's eyes in a green puff of powder. He watched the vines break apart down the entire side of the building. A moment later, they were completely gone, with no trace of them left behind.

Jimmy looked over his shoulder at the super hero. He still hadn't stirred. "Is his pulse back?" Jimmy asked.

Lois felt Superman's neck with her fingers. "No," she said quietly. She gently cradled the Man of Steel's face in her hands. "Wake up, Superman! Please wake up!"

"Hello, Lois," came Superman's raspy voice.

Lois looked down in shock to see the Man of Steel staring up at her.

"I'm fine," Superman said weakly. "Just a little tired."

"You don't look fine," Lois said.

Then Lois suddenly slapped him on the S-shield on his chest. "You scared me!" she cried. "I thought we'd lost you forever."

Jimmy walked over to Superman's side and kneeled beside Lois. "Yeah, you were out for over twenty minutes, big guy," he said.

"Like I said, I'm fine now," said Superman, smiling. "Thanks to both of you, that is."

Superman sat up slowly. "In fact, I'm impressed with both of you," he said. "The way you dealt with Ivy's crooks was brave. And good teamwork."

Jimmy grinned. "Nothing I couldn't handle," he said, slamming his fist into the palm of his other hand.

"All in a day's work," agreed Lois.

"I'm glad you're both okay," Superman said, standing up. He gave Lois and Jimmy one last smile . . . then he leaped out the window!

WOOOOOOOOOOOOOOOOOOSH!

Lois and Jimmy watched Superman fall through the air for a few storeys. Their hearts pounded with fear.

Then the super hero righted himself and rose towards the skyline.

As he disappeared into the sunset, Lois realized that she was smiling a little too much.

"He sure does know how to make an exit," Jimmy said.

Lois nodded. "Yeah," she agreed, "life is never boring when the Man of Steel is around."

*   *   *

An hour later, the police left with Poison Ivy and her gang in custody. As they were leaving, a voice called out from behind them. "Hey, guys! I was stuck in traffic. Did I miss anything?"

Lois turned around to see Clark Kent walk into the newsroom. He nonchalantly made his way over to his desk, adjusted his glasses, and sat down.

"What happened in here?" Clark asked. "I saw police officers leaving the place, and the whole building smells like a greenhouse."

"Are you even serious, Smallville?" Lois said. "Did you not just see who jumped out the –"

RING! RING! The phone on Lois's desk rang. She picked it up. After a second, she put her hand over the speaker and yelled, "Perry!"

Perry White rushed out of his office and into the newsroom. "Yeah?" he asked.

"It's the printer," Lois said. "They say they found a paper stock that should work for us. It's made from 100% recycled paper. Should I tell them to forget about it?"

Perry White seemed to be lost in thought for a second.

"You know what, that'll be fine," Perry said. "Let's go ahead with the change."

"What was that call about, Boss?" Clark asked. Perry didn't answer. He walked back into his office.

Lois grinned. "Looks like we're going green after all," she said.

"Hey, Kent," boomed Perry's voice from his office door. "No more long lunches, you hear? I've got enough expenses paying for fancy paper now, so I can't afford any freeloaders."

"Yes, Mr White," Clark said. He sat down at his desk and turned on his computer. There was a dried leaf on his keyboard.

Clark brushed it off onto the floor, and got back to work.

POISON IVY

Real Name:
Pamela Isley

Occupation:
Botanist, Criminal

Base:
Gotham City

Height:
1.67 metres

Weight:
50 kilograms

Eyes:
Green

Hair:
Chestnut

Pamela Isley was born with immunities to plant toxins and poisons. Her love of plants began to grow like a weed at an early age. She eventually became a botanist (plant scientist). Through reckless experimentation with various flora, Pamela Isley's skin itself has become poisonous. Her venomous lips and plant weapons present a real problem for crime fighters. But Ivy's most dangerous quality is her extreme love of nature – she cares more about the smallest seed than any human.

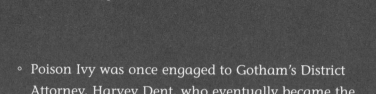

- Poison Ivy was once engaged to Gotham's District Attorney, Harvey Dent, who eventually became the super-villain Two-Face! Their relationship ended when Dent built a prison on a field of wildflowers.

- Poison Ivy emits toxic fragrances that can be harmful to humans. Whenever she is locked up in Arkham Asylum, a wall of Plexiglas must separate her from the guards to ensure their safety.

- Ivy may love her plant creations, but that love hasn't always been returned. A man-eating plant of her own design became self-aware. The thing called itself Harvest and turned on Ivy.

- Ivy's connection to plants is so strong that she can control them by thought alone.

BIOGRAPHIES

MATTHEW K. MANNING is the author of many books and comics, from *The Batman Files* to single issues of comic books such as Looney Tunes. He recently penned a mini-series for DC Comics, and is developing another new original series. He lives in Connecticut, USA, with his wife, Dorothy, and his daughter, Lillian.

LUCIANO VECCHIO was born in 1982 and currently lives in Buenos Aires, Argentina. With experience in illustration, animation, and comics, his works have been published in the UK, Spain, USA, France and Argentina. Credits include *Ben 10* (DC Comics), *Cruel Thing* (Norma), *Unseen Tribe* (Zuda Comics) and *Sentinels* (Drumfish Productions).

GLOSSARY

creep move very slowly and quietly

enhanced improved, better or greater

familiar well known, or easily recognizable

henchman thug or criminal under the employ of a leader

hoarse rough and sore

humid damp and moist

incapacitated unable to move, act or respond

infused joined with something else

overgrown something that has grown due to a lack of supervision such as a garden with many weeds

penitentiary prison for people found guilty of serious crimes

scrambled rushed or struggled to get somewhere or get something

weariness being tired or fatigued

DISCUSSION QUESTIONS

1. What are some ways that you can help stop global warming, or climate change? Write down a list of things to recycle, ways to save energy and how to protect nature.

2. Superman gets a lot of help from his friends, Lois and Jimmy, in this book. What are some things they did to help? Find as many as you can.

3. This book has ten illustrations. Which one is your favourite? Why?

WRITING PROMPTS

1. Superman and Poison Ivy both want to improve the world they live in, but they go about it in very different ways. What are the differences in their actions? Why is Superman a hero, and Ivy a villain? Write about it.

2. For much of this book, Superman is weakened by Kryptonite and can't use his superpowers. Write your own story about Superman without his powers. How does he stop the criminal, or save the day, without his powers? You decide!

3. Write a letter to the *Daily Planet* as a concerned citizen. In your letter, try to convince the newspaper to switch to recycled paper.